MARGRET & H. A. REY's

Curious George

and the Birthday Surprise

WALKER BOOKS

AND SUBSIDIARIES

LONDON • BOSTON • SYDNEY • AUCKLAND

First published in Great Britain 2006
by Walker Books Ltd, 87 Vauxhall Walk, London SE11 5HJ

6 8 10 9 7

© 2003 Houghton Mifflin Company
Curious George® is a registered trademark of Houghton Mifflin Company
Published by arrangement with Houghton Mifflin Company

This book has been typeset in Gill Sans MT Schoolbook
Illustrated in the style of H. A. Rey by Martha Weston

Printed in China

British Library Cataloguing in Publication Data:
a catalogue record for this book is available from the British Library

ISBN 978-1-4063-0037-6

www.walker.co.uk

This is George.

He was a good little monkey and always very curious.

"Today is a special day," the man with the yellow hat told George

at breakfast. "I have a surprise planned and lots to do to get ready.

You can help me by staying out of trouble."

George was happy to help.

Later, while George was looking out the window (and being very good), he heard some tinkly music. It was coming from an ice cream van! George watched as a whole line of children and their dogs enjoyed some ice cream treats.

It looked like fun.

But when the ice cream van moved on, George forgot all about
staying out of trouble and went to find some fun of his own.

In the living room George found party blowers ...

and hats ...

and games!

Could this be part of his friend's surprise?

Before George could find out, he spotted some streamers, balloons and coloured tissue. He could not resist...

Decorating was easy
for a little monkey!

Still, George was curious about the surprise.
And what was that good smell coming from
the kitchen? George followed his nose.

9

Mmmm. It was a cake! And it looked as good as it smelled. All it needed was some icing. George had seen his friend make icing before.

But today his friend was busy.
Maybe George could help.
He could ice the cake himself!

First George put a bit of this
in the mixing bowl.
Next he added a bit of that.
Then he turned the mixer on.

The icing whirled
around and around.

It was whirling too fast! But when George tried to stop the mixer it only went faster

and faster

and FASTER!

George lifted the beaters out of the bowl. Icing flew everywhere!

Poor George. He did not mean to make such a mess. He had only wanted to help. Now how could he clean up the sticky kitchen?

Just then George heard the tinkly music again. The ice cream

van was coming back up the street, and George had

an idea. Quickly he opened the door...

and invited all of the dogs in for a treat!

In no time, the kitchen was as clean as a whistle.

When the dogs finished their snack, George took them back outside. The ice cream van was still there. And so was his friend!

"George!" said the man with the yellow hat. "I've been looking for you. It's time for the surprise!"
George had found hats, games, decorations and a cake.
He was curious.
Was the surprise a party?

Yes! It was a party! George was happy to see all of his friends. They were glad to see George, too. "What great decorations," Bill said. "What a lot of presents!" said Betsy.

"Why don't you play some games with the guests, George?" the man with the yellow hat suggested. "I have one more thing to do."

When George's friend came back he was carrying a cake covered
in candles. This wasn't just any party. It was a birthday party!
But George was still curious. Whose birthday was it?
He watched to see who would
blow out the candles.

The man with the yellow hat put the cake down right
in front of George. That was a surprise! It was George's
birthday. The party was for him! Everyone sang "Happy Birthday".
Then George took a deep breath ...

and made a wish.

"Happy birthday, George!"